Message

from an

Ancestor

Margarette Joyner

MESSAGE FROM AN ANCESTOR
Margarette Joyner

Published by:
Pecan Tree Publishing
Dania Beach, FL 33004.
www.pecantreebooks.com

For bulk copies after licensing contact:
adminservices@pecantreebooks.com

For licensing, please see the PRODUCTION LICENSING
PAGE, and/or contact:
theartistryofms.m@gmail.com

979-8-9913711-6-2 – Paperback
979-8-9913711-7-9 – Ebook

Cover Art by: Mujika (Mujika Graphics and Illustrations)
Cover and Interior Design by: Jenette Sityar

Dedication

To my Ancestors
For passing down a legacy of elegance,
royalty and grace, thank you
For orally holding on to our stories so our heritage
could not be erased, thank you
For singing songs of hope that gave us something
to hold on to, thank you
For teaching us that even in the midst of oppression
and pain, love still abides, thank you
For creating a culture that knows the final word
is in the hands of a higher power, thank you
For choosing to survive so that we could continue
the fight, thank you

To my Supporters
For all those who supported me in this journey, thank you

To my Daughter
For always being a steadfast champion
for all my creative endeavors, thank you

I AM
Thank you for choosing me to represent
so much of your work

The world premiere of *Message From A Slave* from which *Message From an Ancestor* was born, was produced by The Heritage Ensemble Theatre Company in February 2017.

Cast and Crew

CHAKU/AYO	Pamela Archer Shaw
DIRECTOR	Shanea N. Taylor
PRODUCTION MANAGER	Shalandis Wheeler Smith
SET AND LIGHTING DESIGN	Vinnie Gonzalez
COSTUME DESIGNER	Margarette Joyner
MUSIC AND SOUND DESIGN	Earlie K. Joyner
STAGE MANAGER	Kevonnie Shelton

ADDITIONAL PERFORMANCES

Selected reading, 2022 Garland Thompson, Sr. Readers Series at the **National Black Theatre Festival** in Winston Salem, N.C.

Selected reading, 2023 **Pacific Northwest Multi-Cultural (PNMC) Readers Series & Film Festival** in Portland, Oregon.

Characters

Chaku (Mattie): A 20+ year old enslaved woman
Ayo (Sally): Chaku's 100+ year old daughter
Chaku Translator (Black female, can be Ayo): Offstage
Auctioneer (White male): Offstage

Setting

A coat rack, boxes of all sizes for standing on and sitting, trees, African artifacts, carvings, bigger than life wooden silhouettes of: African mother, 3 Warriors (one standing tall, one standing but smaller than the other, one kneeling with his hands up), and one of an Overseer with a gun. Mud cloth/ African fabrics all about the stage. Act 2, remove Overseer silhouette and place rocking chair center stage.

Time

19th Century/Now

Scene Breakdown - ACT 1
Scene 1 – The Welcome
Scene 2 – An Introduction
Scene 3 – The Capture
Scene 4 – The Ship
Scene 5 – The Block
Scene 6 – The Warrior
Scene 7 – Kinchasa
Scene 8 – The Fight
Scene 9 – The Lynching

Scene Breakdown – ACT 2

Sound Effects and Music Placement

ACT 1

Scene 1 *(Suggested African chant)*
Funga Alafia
Auctioneer
Chaku translation

Scene 2
Ocean against wood (sfx)
African percussion (celebratory and message invoking, sfx)
African Village Chanting (sfx)

Scene 3
The Ship, original piece by the playwright

Scene 8
Whip

Scene 9
Gunshot (sfx)

ACT 2

Scene 1 *(Suggested)*
Ain't That Good News, Negro spiritual
Sometimes I Feel Like A Motherless Child, Negro spiritual
Down by The Riverside, Negro spiritual

Scene 3 *(Suggested)*
Wade in The Water, Negro spiritual

Scene 7 *(Suggested)*
Every Day'll Be Sunday, Negro hymn

Costuming

For the premier of this production, Chaku wore a colorful African print lappa (wrap skirt), bralette and headdress all made of the same fabric. She changed into a 19th century dress that an enslaved female would have worn with a head rag. She did not wear shoes for either outfit. Ayo wore an oversized white gown (grand bubba), white shoes and a white mob cab. She also carried an African cane that was made by Matthew.

ADDITIONAL PRODUCTION NOTES

The actor portraying Chaku should have a Yoruba dialect that can be clearly understood. So, a hint of it will suffice. She should also be able to speak Kiswahili when speaking for Kinchasa. She also needs to be a fearless storyteller, who knows how to tell a compelling story and live that story in front of an audience.

The song "The Ship" is an original composition written by the playwright that is sung acapella. Melody coaching can be provided directly by the playwright.

ACT 1

SCENE 1

CHAKU

> Enters through the audience
> singing something like Funga
> Alafia. When she reaches the
> center front of the audience,
> she begins to speak in her
> native tongue but realizes the
> audience can't understand
> her.

CHAKU

O dara ojo awon ololufe me!

VOICEOVER

Good day my loved ones!

CHAKU

O dara pupo lati wa niwaju re!

VOICEOVER

It is so good to be in your presence!

CHAKU

O lewa!

VOICEOVER

You are beautiful!

CHAKU

Oh, oh o ko ye me?

VOICEOVER

You don't understand me?

> She then reaches to the
> heavens and asks for
> translation so the people can
> here in their native tongue
> and a voiceover asks the
> same question in English.

CHAKU

Eleda

VOICEOVER

Creator

CHAKU

Fun mi ni agbara lati yi ede Yoruba me pada si ede ti awon omo re le gbo.

VOICEOVER

Grant me the ability to change my Yoruba tongue to a language your children can understand.

CHAKU

Good day my loved ones! It is so good to be in your presence. You are beautiful! You are African and you're sitting here as free as our ancestors were in our homeland. I did not think I would ever see the day. Tell me something, what are you doing with your freedom?

> She puts up her hand to stop
> them from answering.

You need not give me an answer now. Just something for you to think about. I never thought I'd see this day. I've been waiting a long time to come here and talk to you. You see, I and all your other ancestors have been watching over you. And you know what? You are doing well! But you know what else? You could be doing better. Many of you could do more for one another if you had a mind to, but you do not. Why? Is it because a great deal of you have put yourselves before your brother or your sister? Well, that is what I want to talk to you about today. And I suppose I should start by introducing myself.

> She runs onto the stage

SCENE 2

I was born Chaku, which means sweet, self-sufficient, powerful, courageous, visionary, and cunning. I come from Abomey, a little village in Africa in the country of Benin. It was the capital of Dahomey where Kings lived for many years. One of whom was my father, King Agonglo who inherited a failing economic kingdom from his father.

During his reign he reformed economic policies and led many military expeditions. We lived richly, as my father was a cunning political strategist and benefited greatly in the slave trade. Of course, we had no knowledge that slavery across the water was different from what it was in our country.

You see, my father's enslaved people, who were captives from other villages, served with their labor for a certain amount of time and then were adopted into our tribe or were released once they had served their time. We owned their labor, not their minds. My mother, a Dutch African Queen, taught me everything I know about walking in one's power.

She was with me through the second phase of my initiation, which are rituals that guide us to our life's mission. There are five stages in total: birth, adulthood, marriage, eldership and ancestorship. During this second phase, I was taught about society, given moral instruction and clarification of my calling in life which was to follow in my father's path.

After my training, I welcomed my time sitting by the water quietly listening for the answer to the questions I had, even at the tender age of fifteen. I know what my elders saw for me, but I often dreamt of traveling the world learning about different cultures and studying many languages. Do not misunderstand, I loved my community and can remember my homeland vividly.

Trees were tall and wide with branches that hung low like arms reaching down to hug you. My favorite tree to sit under while contemplating was the baobab tree whose trunk is large, smooth, and shiny. I loved how the roots stuck up into the air like they had been planted upside down. The sky was clear, and the water was deeper than the deepest blue.

You could step out into the ocean and see the creatures traveling to whatever destination they were headed to. One day, there was a celebration happening after several of us had completed our rites of adulthood.

Drums begin to play, and we
can hear the chants of the
village.

The drums were beating and everyone, everywhere was
dancing, laughing with abandon and having a glorious time.

The music rises and she does
an African dance.

Me and Baraka, that's the boy I was sweet on, sneaked off
and was sitting by the water talking, holding hands, and
kissing like we always did. Now don't get any peculiar ideas
because that's all we did. We'd hold hands and kiss because
we were not allowed to do anything else until we were
united. My mama would always tell me, "iyen ni ohun-ini re
ti o niye julo mase fi fun enikeni, o je ki won jo'gun re." That
is your most precious possession. You don't give it away to
anyone, you make them earn it.

(She warns the audience)

Take heed. Anyhow, me and Baraka were sitting there, and
I can remember just like it was yesterday, the sun was about
to set just above the horizon and there was a cool breeze
blowing off the water. I was sitting in front of him, and his
arms and legs were wrapped around me as the rest of him
cradled me. Our fingers were entwined, and I could feel the
warmth of his breath on my neck as he spoke.

We were there talking about our dreams of traveling the
world together and becoming great scholars. We dreamt of
the day we would join as one and spoke of the generations
we would contribute to with our children. Suddenly, we
heard the rumblings of our people. The rhythm of the drums
shifted, and an uneasiness came over me.

My heartbeat increased, and I could feel Baraka's heart pounding against my back. We quickly rose to our feet when the drums came to an abrupt silence. The voices of our loved ones grew loud, then louder and louder. We saw our families running in every direction as dirt formed clouds around them. Then we saw people that were the color of wheat, running behind them.

Some of our kinsmen were being slaughtered right before our eyes. My father and mother being among them. They fought gallantly like the warriors they were, but in the end their lives were taken. Baraka and I were in such horror, we could not move and before we could gather our senses to run toward our people to help, the wheat people came from behind.

Two men grabbed me, and two others grabbed Baraka, and they pulled us apart. We fought with all our might, but their strength in numbers were greater than our might and we were defeated. I was so frightened, not so much of them, but of the evil that was behind their eyes. As they dragged us away, I held on to Baraka's hand for as long as I could, knowing in my heart that I might never feel him again.

SCENE 3

My hands were tied in front of me as we were dragged to the edge of the shore. They put us in our own small boats, my father's boats. I recognized one of the men who had negotiated trades with him. When our eyes locked, I knew he recognized me as well since my father often allowed me to be present at their meetings.

This man had sat at our table and supped with us. How could he practice such betrayal? I screamed at him in his language, "Why?!" One of his men raised his weapon to strike me, but the man I knew put up his hand to stop the blow and approached his man. He whispered something in his ear, looked down at me, smiled triumphantly and went about his business.

Where were they taking us? How could this be? I could see two large ships in the distance. I had seen them before as my father made much of his wealth by trading goods with England. Fruits that were exotic to them but common for us, shells, cloth. What I did not know was that the main cargo in the ships awaiting us was that of other tribes.

As we came closer to them the atmosphere seemed to thicken. Baraka was put on one ship, and I was put on the other. We were bound together by the neck with rope in groups of ten or so, then loaded onto the ship. It was as monstrous as what I saw in their eyes. Our men were separated from us, and although I'd known fear while being stalked by an animal, I had never known fear like this.

I closed my eyes and stopped breathing as they ripped the royal garments from my body. The beads I wore that were meant to bring wisdom, hope and well-being were grabbed carelessly from my neck. They were given to me by my father and so it felt as if part of me and him were being torn away. They probed and prodded, looked and laughed, some moaned and groaned with lust dripping from their lips.

Our men were thrown into the belly of the monstrous beast and we; the women were put just below deck. I could hear the language of different tribes, the Fulani, the Igbo, and the

Asante crying out. They piled us so close, two of us could not turn around at the same time.

The stench made our stomachs weak as we inhaled blood, excrement, and death. We were chained yet, they beat us, mocked us, spat on us, and called us names many did not understand. But I understood. Not just by their words, I could read their eyes.

On one hand they were treating us like animals and the next minute they were taking bodies to do with as they pleased. And not just the women, they took our men and young boys as well. But some of them would not be taken. Instead, they would fight to the death or throw themselves overboard involuntarily taking those that were tied to them as well.

Others would return with glazed over eyes having lost their reason, their minds. Some women were repeatedly taken, while the rest of us did all we could to drown out their screams as they were being brutalized. We sang and called out their names so they would know we were with them. For some reason unbeknownst to me, I and others were spared.

We sailed for what seemed like an eternity and the sight of our homeland ceased with every passing day. No more clear water, no more dreams, no more baobab trees. Every day we were taken to the top deck to get fresh air and to dance for our captor's pleasure. But the dancing here had no meaning.

So, we did not lift our feet far from the ground because there was nothing to celebrate. There was no story we wanted to tell through our movements. Instead, the deck was an opportunity for those of us who chose to live, to breathe fresh air.

Every day, there were fewer of us which did give us room to move, but it was of little comfort. Every movement caused suffering from the wounds we bore not only from the beatings with the leather stringed whip, but from our skin constantly scraping against the wooden planks at the ship's sway. Some chose starvation, some died of diseases they acquired from the captors and those that were elder who had gone through four stages of initiation in the village would simply close their eyes and cease to be, taking them to their final initiation stage of ancestorship.

At first there was a great deal of wailing whenever the doors would open. We wailed for the ones who chose death and for the ones who had no choice since they were bound to the choosers. We wailed for the virtue that was taken, but mostly we wailed for the unknown. After weeks of this, many of us determined that no matter what they did to us, we would not break. So, we laid there, some wondering aloud what we had done to deserve this. Some asked if we were being punished for not taking the Elders seriously when they warned us that unrest would soon come.

Others questioned if we had gotten so prideful in our conquests or if we were too comfortable in our wealth? Why did we trust them enough to open ourselves up to this? Is that why the Creator seemed to have turned His back on us and closed His ears to our cries? No answers came and so the eldest among us told us to listen to the ocean for answers. But most of us had not reached that level of initiation and could not hear. I tried to sing my sorrows away, but like my tears, even that was fading away with time. For days and nights to come, we were repeatedly punished, breathed death, and felt the sway of the slave ship.

She sits up and remembers.
The stage lights change to
a blue wash, and we hear
sounds of the ocean. She is
almost in silhouette as she
sings.

THE SHIP

WE WERE PUT AWAY ON THE SHIP BOUND AND
GAGGED
BABY'S DEAD
THE SHIP, I SHALL NEVER, I NEVER WILL FORGET
MY SISTERS DIED
WARRIORS CRIED
ON THE SHIP OF OPPRESSION AND I NEVER, I
NEVER WILL
FORGET

AS THE HORROR ROSE
I COULD HARDLY BREATH
DEATH ALL AROUND ME
A GRAVY FORMED BENEATH
IN THE BELLY, BELLY OF THE BEAST

WE WERE ON THE SHIP OF OPPRESSION
AND THE CONSTANT PRAYER FROM I
LORD, LET ME DIE

SCENE 4

We had not been up for air for several days, so when the doors opened one morning, the sun shone so bright it hurt our eyes as we climbed the stairs. The ship was no longer moving for some reason. Out of the hundreds we began with, only about half remained. Small boats were waiting, and we were taken ashore. We were now in a strange land where there were more wheat people than we had ever seen.

You know, like the ones that took us, only their language was different. I don't know how to describe it, there was a laziness to it, and it was quite offensive to our ears. Everything was moving fast, too fast for us. In our homeland, our steps were ordered by purpose, and we walked with pride, but it was not possible as we were pushed and herded past hungry eyes.

Some covered their mouths with cloth but could not hide their greed. They put us in a holding place that was large and smelled of animals. They dashed buckets of water on us to clean us up. They said we had the smell of death on us. I suppose so. Sometimes our deceased brothers and sisters would be in the belly of the beast for a long time before someone would come and get them to throw them overboard.

So, the water was welcoming to me because just for a moment, it reminded me of home. It reminded me of running on the shoreline with Baraka and feeling the coolness of water splashing on my body with every step. I closed my eyes and for a brief moment, I felt a bit of relief.

Over the journey I and others had deciphered a bit more of the wheat people's language and had learned to communicate with one another, even if but by gestures. So, we understood when they threw garments at us and told us to put them on and ordered us to stay as they untied us.

She puts on slavery clothing.

By then we were so relieved to not be in the water, most of us just laid down and went to sleep. Well, some slept, some kept watch. It was their calling at home to protect, warn, pray, and in this place they did the same. Early the next morning, just after the sun rose, another group of Africans were brought in.

They looked even more worn than we did, and we found out that they were from the other ship. We could see it whenever we were brought up for air, but lost sight of it after some time. When they came in and the doors were shut, I heard them whispering out names, like they were desperately looking for someone they knew.

Imamu! Spiritual leader. Akua! Wednesday born. Babatunde! Return of the father. And just before I could call out, I heard my name. Chaku, Chaku. When I turned toward the voice, I saw his face. It was Baraka. I ran to him and threw my arms around him, holding on for strength.

He whispered, "ifemi, ifemi. My love, my love." He took my face in his hands and kissed me as tears rolled down our faces. We touched, lovingly and asked one another, "se od da? Are you alright?" He was so thin. Then he told of the stop they had made and explained why there were only a few of them.

He said, "We were taken ashore, and they put us on display for people who examined every inch of our bodies. Some fought choosing death over captivity. Our sister, Binsa, who was of great beauty used her fingernails to scar her face in hopes they would not want her.

But the men were undeterred by that and bid a great sum for her. When her bidder pulled her to him, he did not try to hide his lust. She pushed away from him and shouted, "jagunjagun!! Jagunjagun!" Warrior!! Warrior! and then spat at him. With one blow from the butt of his weapon, she transitioned with a smile upon her face. Others surrendered to the purchasers and were carted off in wagons.

I had refused to eat and was weakened during the journey, so I was not sold and put back on the ship." All had become quiet as we listened and watched as he spoke. We were astonished at this story, and I could feel yet another kind of fear and before I could recover from what I'd just heard, the door of the shed opened.

And that is when the realization of what had just been described was about to happen to me. Three men brandishing weapons walked among us probing and prodding and then stopped in front of me. And just like before, the last thing I saw of Baraka was his hand leaving mine. They snatched me from him and took me outside.

There were mostly men in the front of the crowd with a few pale women in the back and on the sides. None of them spoke. They scoffed as I was led through them, and I could feel hands touching me as I passed. I wanted to scream, I wanted to fight, yet I wanted to live. They put me on the block, and I could see Baraka standing in the shed and we locked eyes. I saw his breath bring him into his fullness as his chest swelled and his shoulders dropped. It gave me strength to come into mine.

My chest swelled, my shoulders dropped, and I held my head high looking at no one but him. I stood strong and proud; and called on the ancestors. Nabulungi! Zuberi! Agonglo! They stepped forward and I began to pray.

> Auction chant voiceover with the sounds of the buyers as background.

CHAKU

Creator!

AUCTIONEER VOICEOVER

Ladies and gentlemen! This next wench is a fine specimen. She is lusty in all areas of the body and has childbearing hips.

CHAKU

Give me strength.

AUCTIONEER VOICEOVER

She is a fresh cargo coming from the coast of Africa where her people were of great wealth.

CHAKU

Creator!

AUCTIONEER VOICEOVER

As you can see, her face is pleasant to look upon and she has good teeth.

> She opens her mouth.

AUCTIONEER VOICEOVER

I'll start the bidding at three hundred pounds. Step up gentleman and take a closer look!

CHAKU

Give me strength Father.

AUCTIONEER VOICEOVER

If you feel her arms and legs, you'll see she is strong and will make a fine field hand.

CHAKU

Let your mercy and goodness surround me so I will not fear what comes against me.

AUCTIONEER VOICEOVER

Three hundred pounds is the bid, can I hear four? Three hundred can I hear four? Four hundred to the gentleman in the rear! Four hundred pounds can I hear five. Can I hear five."

CHAKU

Restore my spirit and turn my weakness into strength.

AUCTIONEER VOICEOVER

Turn her around and lift her petticoat so we can get a good look.

She turns around and lifts her dress to just below her butt.

AUCTIONEER VOICEOVER

Five hundred to Mr. Winstone. The bid is five hundred, can I hear six? Five hundred can I hear six?

CHAKU

Give me courage, Father.

AUCTIONEER VOICEOVER

From what I'm told by the ship's captain, this wench was spared, so her body has not been defiled.

CHAKU

Evil has darkened our world, and we need your light. Shine through us and numb us to despair.

AUCTIONEER VOICEOVER

"Six can I hear seven? Seven hundred pounds is the bid! Seven can I hear eight? Can I hear eight? Can I hear eight?"

CHAKU

Let me know your presence is with me always. Cover me Jesu, Ase.

AUCTIONEER VOICEOVER

Having heard no other bids, she is sold to Mr. Chauncy.

SCENE 5

And just like that I was sold off. Some men snatched me from the block and tied my hands in front of me, then took me to their wagon. As the wagon began moving, I walked alongside it, alone. That is how I ended up on the Chauncy Plantation. Captain Jonathan P. Chauncy paid 700 pounds for me and all the while I was with him, he said I was the worst purchase he had ever made. I gave them so much trouble. I would not let them treat me like they did many of the other women.

After the day's work was done and the sun went down, the overseers and patrollers would begin their late-night hunt. Most times, I could find hiding places to stay out of their reach. They would take wives, mothers, sisters, sons, children to the woods in the back of the big house and I could hear their screams – then - their silence.

I always remembered what my mother said and since I had escaped the brutalization on the beast, I was determined to keep my virtue. So, when the evil ones would come for me late in the night I could not be found. However, there was one night, one of the overseers and his men came to the slave quarters before I could get away. One of them grabbed me by the hair and another held my arms like this.

> She demonstrates by holding her hands behind her.

I tried hard to fight but there were several of them so I could not break free. He said to me, "Mattie," that's what they called me. "I hear you one of them mean negras that can't be broke. Well, I got news for you gal, you gon' be broke tonight; hehehe." And they laughed loudly, smelling like something had crawled in their bellies and died. They took me out in the back of the big house. The men pushed me down to my knees and the overseer stood in front of me. He said, "Open your mouth and if you bite me, I'm gon' beat you within an inch of your life. But I'm gon' break you tonight gal, now I said open your mouth." I looked at him, rose into the fullness of myself and responded, "yes, master." And then I did as they demanded, I opened my mouth.

> She sings with fervor, a
> song - voodoo-like. When
> she's at the height of it, she
> rises and looks like she is
> cursing each of them.

Carrying on something like that. When I'd finished, they were all just standing there looking at me the way some of you are looking at me now. After that night, they started telling everyone that I had a disordered mind. But I didn't care what they called me as long as they left me be.

SCENE 6

One day, not too long after that, I heard Master Chauncy and his men talking. Unbeknownst to them we were aware of what was and what was to come because we were always in earshot of them speaking. Cooks heard conversations around the dinner table. Field workers heard the overseers discussions, house servants heard all the talking that went on in the house.

They thought we were too ignorant to understand them but what they did not know was that we were avid learners and could quickly master anything we set our minds to. We simply pretended not to know. Master Chauncy said, "That Mattie is a wildcat that's for sho and she do got a mighty strong will, but by God she works harder than any woman I ever seen in my life.

She got more skills than most and got a childbearing body that will bring me more profit once she starts birthing, but we gon' have to do something to tame her." Then one of the other men said, "Why don't we just break her the same way we break the horses. Get her a big, strong buck and make him do the job." And they laughed. Well, I had made up my mind that I was going to do the same thing to my big, strong buck that I did to them.

Several weeks later, I had been out in the field all day long and I was sweaty, smelly, and tired because most days they would work me like they worked the men. Well, just when we were about to end the day, we saw the slave wagon coming up the road. There were only two men on the back of it and about six white men around them. We knew when they came in like that, a warrior was coming that they wanted but also feared. When they passed, I could see one of them was a small man who looked like he would faint any moment.

We later found out he could speak seven languages which made him quite valuable. The other one was big, sat tall, and looked straight ahead. That was the warrior. Not too long after they were out of sight, Master Tom came to me and said Captain Chauncy wanted to see me in the shed.

When I entered, the overseer pulled me by the arm and pushed me down in front of this warrior and Captain Chauncy said, "Unchain him and lock 'em in here for a day or two. Maybe they'll kill each other and save me the trouble of being bothered with either one of 'em."

They closed the door and locked us in. Well, I jumped to my feet and was ready for battle. But it was as if he knew what

I was thinking before I could speak and he said, "Salamu dada yangu. Greetings my sister." "Mimi ni Kinchasa na ninakupa neno langu." My name is Kinchasa, and I give you my word." "Sitawahi kuweka mkono juu yako," I will never put a hand on you," "mpaka ni matakwa yako." Unless it is your wish." And then he sat down. I did not know what to do, so for a moment I just stood there, frozen.

Then I looked into his eyes. Do you know what I saw? Although he bore many scars, which told me he had suffered, I saw his light. I saw truth. And then I saw him.

(Her tone changes)

My gaze began at the crown of his head and scoured the length of his body down to his feet. He was tall and black as the night. His skin had been kissed by the sun and was smooth like a newborn. His hair had twisted itself into long coils that hung past his shoulders. His eyes were deep set, piercing and almost took my breath away as he seemed to look through me. His lips were full like a ripe, juicy, juicy mango.

He had strong, powerful arms and his chest was wide, chiseled and fell into a small waistline. His hands were large, and his legs were like a prize stallion that had never been broken. When I raised my eyes and looked back into his face, I could have drowned in the hint of his smile. I truly thought I would perish where I stood.

Even though I loved Baraka and prayed often that we would one day find one another, I had never felt what was rushing through me at that moment. I truly thought if I did not break my gaze, I would melt right where I stood. But I could not look away. So once again, I looked in his eyes and they said he would not hurt me.

Slowly, I made my way over to him and sat beside him. For two days, we learned to communicate with one another through gestures, tears and even a bit of laughter. And then I slept as he watched over me. When I woke up the next morning, he was holding me in his arms and for the first time since I was stolen from my homeland, I felt safe.

SCENE 7

For months, we would steal away with one another no matter how long the day or how hard the work. He taught me words from his language, and I taught him words from mine, but we needed no words to understand one another. It was only a few months after his arrival did Captain Chauncy allow us to unite. Of course, he did not have much choice seeing as nothing they did could keep us apart.

They would sometimes purposely keep us away from one another as punishment or amusement. But we would always find a way to see one another if only for a moment. Every morning before the back breaking work began, we would pass by each other, touch fingers, and that would be enough to get us through the day. Have you ever been loved like that? Have you ever loved someone so much that when they are not there you ache on the inside for them or thought your heart would explode at the very sight of them? Well, that is how we were.

Our bond was not recognized legally because the law that they created said we were property, not human beings. However, we knew in our hearts what we were, who we were and to whom we really belonged. The day we jumped the broom at a gathering was one of the happiest days of my life. Our communal family had gathered just outside the enslaved quarters. There was drumming and dancing and calling on the ancestors for blessings. The broom, which represents God and family, was decorated with ribbons that symbolizes the ties that bind us together.

Kinchasa stood tall and full of pride as I came to greet him. I took his hand as the preacher gave his advice and blessings. We promised ourselves to one another and together we jumped over the broom. When our feet hit the ground on the other side of it, we were one in the eyes of our community and our God. When he took me in his arms he whispered in his native tongue of Kiswahili, "kwa moyo wanguwote, nakupenda." With my whole heart, I love you." And for every day that he lived I assured him that he too held my heart.

SCENE 8

I shall never forget the last time I saw him. Kinchasa and I had lived in love for four years when one day while in the field, I fell ill. I dropped my basket and began walking toward the slave quarters. I could hear the overseer screeching for me to get back to work. I raised my voice and shouted "No!" I went to the slave quarters and laid down.

Captain Chauncy was told what happened and he had his men to come get me and bring me to him. He had his men take me to the middle of the front yard. They tied rope to my wrists and attached each one to the whipping posts so I could not run. He said he was going to make an example out of me so that the rest of the slaves would know better. One of the other enslaved women, Sukie ran to the field to tell Kinchasa and he came running along with many others.

They were held off by the overseer and his men. Captain Chauncy came out carrying a large whip. Kinchasa shook his head no, as he looked at him and spoke in broken English, "Massa, what she do? What she do, sir?" Captain Chauncy turned quickly facing my warrior with evil in his eyes and bilisi, the devil in his spirit. He said, "I don't answer to you boy, this here is my plantation and I'll be damned if I'm gon' have any of my slaves questioning anything I do." Kinchasa say, "Massa, please, please do not hit her. Hit me, nitachukua adhabu yake, I will take her punishment, I will take her place." Captain Chauncy did not say another word to him, and a hush had fallen over the atmosphere as Kinchasa pleaded, "please sir, please, what must I do? I beg, I beg sir!" Captain Chauncy hollered, "Enough! I don't want to hear no more, now get back Daniel!" That is what he called him, Daniel.

Captain Chauncey walked over to me, circled me, then he stopped. I could feel the heat of his body on the back of my neck. He would inflict his punishment from behind. I looked at my warrior and told him assuredly, "Kinchasa, hold your peace. Hold your peace! If you do not, they will kill you and that I cannot bear. I do not care what they do to me, hold your peace." All the while, Kinchasa was begging, "Please sir, please sir!" Then I looked straight into Captain Chauncy's pale face, stood in my full power, and said, "I can take it!" But Kinchasa continued to shake his head no, and I knew if I did not keep speaking to him, he was not going to survive. Captain Chauncy raised the whip over my head, I took a deep breath and called on the ancestors before he came down across my back.

(Sound of a whip)

"Jesu!"

> She drops down to her knees
> as one of her hands slips out
> of the rope. She is almost
> blinded by the pain.

Kinchasa began to buck like a wild stallion. It was as I thought, he could not bear it. Tears rolled down his face and before I could soothe him, Chauncy raised the whip again. I took in as much air as I could, with my eyes stayed on Kinchasa. "Hold your peace my king, I can take it." The whip came down so hard this time I could hardly make a sound.

> (Sound of the whip).

"Jesu."

> (She groans and drops to
> her lap as her other hand
> becomes free from the rope)

I felt tears rolling down my face, but from the depth of my soul I mustered through trembling teeth, "Kinchasa, hold your peace, hold your peace, I can take it, I can take it." But by now, he was rebelling so, it took four of them to hold him back as he screamed, "Massa! No more, no more. Before God Almighty, I kill thee! I kill thee!" Chauncy acted as if he could no longer hear him. He was in his full power and took pleasure in our pain. Again, he raised the whip high above his head, jumped up and came down across my back.

> The sound of whip and a
> guttural groan is heard as she
> falls prostrate.

This time, my garment split, and I could feel the coolness of blood gushing from my skin. I fell on my face, but managed to whisper, "Kinchasa, hold your peace, I can take it. I can take it." Slowly, I raised up onto my knees, and when I looked into his eyes, I knew it would be the last time I saw him alive. He bent down taking all of the men with him and when he came up, he came up roaring like a bear. Men were flying everywhere.

Before any of them could recover, Kinchasa ran full speed and knocked Captain Chauncy flat on his back. On top of him, Kinchasa wrapped his strong hands around his neck, enraged, choking him hollering, "No more, no more!" The more the patrollers hit and pulled on him the tighter his grip became. Chauncy's lips were turning a dark shade of blue and although they wanted to shoot Kinchasa, they could not because they were afraid they would shoot Captain Chauncy as well.

Panicking, one of the men fired a warning shot, (gunshot) another grabbed a little enslaved girl by the hair and stuck his gun to her temple and hollered, "Daniel, turn him loose or I'm gon' blow a hole in this little negra gal's head big enough for you to walk through. And when I finish with her, I'm gon' do the same thing to Mattie and that's after me and my men get through with her!" Kinchasa turned him loose.

SCENE 9

They took him in the shed where we first met and tied him to one wall. His powerful arms were stretched out, tied to the planks and his feet were bound together with strips of leather. They closed the doors to the shed and would not let me in, so I went to the back of it. I could hardly walk, so some of my sisters helped me. As they nursed my wounds, the overseer beat my Kinshasa with his cat-o-nine-tails. With every strike to him, my wounds seemed to cry. But not once did I hear him scream. And when they thought he was going to die, they would toss salt water on him to inflict more pain in order to wake him so they could beat him some more. Still, they could not break him. There were times his blood would seep through the planks and fall on me. I cherished every drop. My people tried to get me to go back to the quarters, but I could not leave him. He would not transition without knowing I was there. If he was a warrior to the end, my warrior, then I would be his.

At dawn, the overseer came and opened the doors to the shed. Alone, I made my way around to the front and when I looked upon Kinchasa's face, he was unrecognizable.

> She screams in horror and faints, then recovers and rises up to a sitting position.

As I gathered my strength, I once again looked at him. My gaze began at the crown of his head and scoured the length of his body down to his feet. Along with the beating, they had castrated him and put a sign above his head that read, here is your warrior. But I knew that was not my warrior, my warrior was here.
(She indicates her heart)
I grieved so hard that I thought I would make my transition with him. But I knew that I could not. I had another mission to carry out. So, I prayed and asked the Creator to give me the strength I needed. He did. Six months later our legacy came. I gave birth to our daughter. I called her Ayo. It means joy. It means joy.

> She exits holding the baby softly singing Funga Alafia.

ACT 2

SCENE 1

SALLY (AYO)

> AYO enters singing a Negro
> hymn/spiritual similar to
> "Ain't That Good News".
> Her rocking chair is placed
> center stage, and the Overseer
> silhouette is gone. Ayo
> crosses to her rocking chair
> when the song is over.

She was right. The Lord did give her strength. She held on until she gave birth to me and then she gave up the ghost. She was 20 years old when she had me. They tell me she didn't die from complications of carrying me like the white folks said, but that she really died from a broken heart. I sure wish I could have gotten to know her. It's one thing to be cared for and loved by others. But there's something about a mother's love that just can't be replaced. I didn't think I could miss something that I never had. But while I was growing up, I could see what that type of love looked like when I saw mothers in our community holding their children. There was a bond that I longed for. Now don't get me wrong, I had folks all around me that loved on me, fed me when I was hungry and comforted me when I was sad. But there was always a part of me that wished my mama was there to look at me the way others were looked upon. Even now, after all these years, I still miss her.

AYO sings a mournful hymn/
song similar to Sometimes I
Feel Like a Motherless Child.

I hear she was something else. Guess that's where I get it
from. My Matthew said that's one of the things he loved
most about me. He'd say I had fire! I sure wish she could
have met Matthew. I believe she would have loved him
just as much as I do. Folks say he reminded them of my
daddy. I was glad to hear that cause everybody talked
about how good of a man my daddy was. Wish I could've
met him too.

When I first laid eyes on Matthew, I knew he was the one
for me. He was just as sweet as he could be. I don't believe
God ever made a better man than him. And he'd always
say the same thing about me. Course he didn't always feel
that way. At first, he didn't pay me no mind at all. 'Til one
Sunday morning, we was at the meeting house. That's where
we could go and get the whole truth of what the bible says
instead of just the passages the white folks wanted us to hear.
Like, "slaves obey your master." And back then we couldn't
call them churches because the preachers weren't teaching
according to the doctrine of the Church of England, which
was used to justify slavery.

Well on this particular morning, the Holy Ghost got a hold of
him and hit him in the top of his head. Must have come out
of his foots, cause he jumped up and went to dancing all over
that gathering. Like to to'e up everything! Folks was getting
all out the way 'cause he was a big man, and I guess some of
them thought they were gon' get hurt but I wasn't worried. I
knowed the Lord had him. You know when the Lord got you,

can't nothing, or nobody bring no harm to you. Well, I tell you, it seemed like he praised the Lord all day long.

Folks had long gone, even the Preacher was gone but I stayed right there. I figure if the holy ghost had me like that, it would be mighty sad to come to and find that no one was around to see me through. So, I stayed. And when he had released all he needed to, he sat down next to me and cried like a baby. We jumped the broom at one of our gatherings just a few weeks later. Now the broom jumping ceremony was something we did because the law didn't legally recognize our marriages. But we knew that as long as God knew our hearts, that's all that really mattered. So, we gathered with our community and the preacher. On the ground was the same decorated broom that my mama and daddy had jumped over. The elders held on to it just for me. I felt blessed to have that particular broom because it felt like they were right there with me.

Well, me and Matthew stood on one side of it and once we got our blessings from the preacher, we grabbed hands and jumped over into a life of togetherness. Afterward, we danced, sang, ate, and thanked God for just a few moments to be able to lay down our burden and enjoy what freedom must have felt like.

> She sings a song like
> "Down by the Riverside"
> and seemingly dances with
> Matthew.

SCENE 2

Yes Lord! We stayed together for 75 years. Folks used to ask me, Sally, that's what my master called me. They'd say, how in the world you stay with one man all them years. I'd tell them, the key word in that question is man. If he wasn't one, I couldn't have stayed with him.

(She chuckles)

My Matthew was what folks would call a softhearted man. He cared deeply for anything that meant something to him. I saw him care for a little bird that had somehow gotten one of his wings hurt and that man patiently got it to trust him and nursed that little creature until he could fly away on his own. For a long time, that bird would stop by every now and again to say hello to him. It stopped coming when Mathew made his transition.

(beat)

He had a deep voice you know but it sounded soft even when he was angry. That didn't happen often unless he thought somebody was bothering me. That's when they found out how strong he was. But more than anything he had a respect for me that let me know I could trust him and that kept my mind at ease.

I used to catch him just looking at me sometimes and without saying a word I heard his eyes telling me he loved me and that made my heart smile. You see, even though I never got the chance to know my daddy, I know from the stories that have been passed down about him, that he loved my mama with all his heart. He too, I'm told, was soft spoken, but also had a rage that would have folks trembling in their boots. Especially when it came to anybody bothering my mama. So, I knowed to wait for a strong man to come find me cause I'm a strong woman and I needed someone that could handle it and not hurt me because of it.

I didn't need just strength in the body, but in the spirit as well. And I didn't have to look for him, I knew God would send me who I needed, when I was ready to receive him. I saw with that little bird and that day in the gathering house how much love was in my Matthew, and I knew.

SCENE 3

I'll tell you something else about my Matthew. The Lord give him a gift. I tell you that man could take a piece of wood and turn it into a thing of sheer beauty right before your eyes. See, one of his jobs was to gather wood for the big house.

Old Captain Chauncy who was bent in the body by the time we jumped the broom, made a deal with Matthew saying if he got the wood every night, he could keep all that didn't fit in the fireplace. We wasn't supposed to know any better, but we knew that was one of his little ways of trying to make up for all the sorrow he had caused me.

You see, like my mama, I can read people's eyes; guilt ate him up until the day he paid his debt to nature. You see after he killed my daddy, they say his heart softened toward everybody, especially me. I used to wonder why he would give me little things. I was a seamstress on the plantation and made the clothes for all the enslaved people on the property.

Most times he would provide the same old rough cloth he always did, but every now and again he would have one of his girls bring me something special and the girl would say, "daddy said this piece is just for you, but keep it between us."

Anyhow, every night after Matthew completed his quota for the day, he would bring home three or four pieces of wood and he'd put up two or three pieces so we would have some to keep warm and cook with, then he'd go to work on the one piece that was left. I tell you, sometimes he wouldn't get through 'til way in the morning. Especially if he'd had a hard day 'cause most days we'd work from dusk till dawn and carving was his release. I'd sit right there with him with my sewing and watch him work.

Sometimes we'd talk about why God didn't see fit to bless us with any children of our own and in the end he'd say, "the way I see it, we been blessed with a whole lot of children and you of all people know it takes all of us to make sure they get to know love, no matter where it come from, before reality takes their breath away."

Sometimes we wouldn't say anything at all, and it was during those times I'd look up from my sewing and catch him looking at me with that beautiful smile in his eyes. Other times I'd sing to him while he carved.

> She sings a Negro classic
> spiritual similar to, "Wade in
> the Water"

All this you see around here, that's my Matthew. The last thing he made for me was this here cane. The way he would caress a piece of wood and show respect for the fact that it had given itself over to him kept me in awe. Sometimes after

Sunday gatherings folks would walk over to our place in the quarters just to see what he had done. And he'd always give somebody something before the day was gone. But most of the best times of my life was spent with just me and him.

(She chuckles)

I used to love for him to wash my hair cause I always had thick hair that felt like another chore when I did it. One day he asked me if I wanted him to do it. I said, "what you know about washing somebody's hair? He said, "I ain't got to know about somebody's hair, all I need to know is about yours." Well, when he washed it the first time, I didn't have any more questions. He could get down to the root and seem like to me, scrub all my troubles away. He used to love to do it too. Said it made him feel good to see the peace that would come over my face while he did it.

(She chuckles)

Used to call me wooly head. Now that made me kind of warm and he knowed it too. Wooly head!

(She chuckles)

Lord that man was something else.

SCENE 4

Let me tell y'all something. Times was hard most of the time, but sometimes believe it or not, it was good even on the plantation. You see, even though most of us had no family with the same blood line, we created families that loved one another. We were never alone. If one needed food, the cooks would find a way to meet their needs.

Those in the house kept us informed, elders soothed aching bodies and children that had been left alone were taken care of by the community. We took care of one another. So, I say it was good in some ways, because if you got yourself some folks that love you, it ain't nothing you can't make it through. That's how all of us made it and not just through slavery, but through freedom too.

When we was freed in 1865, it was one of the best and worst days of our lives! We heard the mistress shouting, "No, no, what will we do?" Then word spread fast that the President had declared us free. Matthew looked at me and I looked at him. At first, we didn't know how to feel and then a lightness came over me. I walked out the door and stepped out into the yard. It was a new step. The sun was shining bright, and I just closed my eyes and let it envelope me for a time. Then I felt Matthew's arms reach from behind me around my waist and we laughed long and hard.

(She laughs)

I turned to him, and he wrapped me in his arms, picked me up and hollered, "We's free!" We went back into the house, threw some things in bags, and talked about what we would do, where we would go. But after the jubilance died down, we realized we didn't have any of the answers. You see, on the plantation, there was food, shelter, and community. But after the war, we found that we were just as powerless as we were when we were in bondage. Most were as illiterate as their owners and unaware of what it was like out there in the world.

We were oppressed by the laws, scared of the Klansmen, and abandoned by the very folks that fought for our freedom. So, plenty of fieldhands became sharecroppers, house slaves became cooks or maids and took in laundry in the evenings. All of whom were taken advantage of when it came to wages under the thumb of a "master like" white person.

Me and Matthew had gotten up in age and had never been outside the plantation so when young Master Chauncy and Mistress asked us to stay on and said they would give us a wage, we stayed. Several other families stayed as well. We were frowned on by some, some understood, and others were just ready to go. But it would be centuries before we would recover from that horrible institution created out of greed. That's the reason I come to talk to you today and I'm gon' get right to the point because I'm old and I ain't got as much energy as I used to have.

SCENE 5

First of all, I want y'all to know that me and your ancestors have been watching over you and in plenty ways, y'all been doing pretty good. However, there are a few things y'all done plum got away from, like how to take care of children. See, what was passed down to us was the way children were raised in The Motherland and that's why we knew how to raise ours.

In Africa, the children were raised by way of rites of passage which were fundamental to their growth. These rites were established by ancestors while they yet lived to link the child to the community and the community to the spirit world. The beginning was the rite of birth, and that was the gift that God blessed the world with and the gift we thanked God for. That's when the babies got their names, and their names had meaning like Ife which means love. Or Jabari which means brave.

They were given names that matched their personalities. They believed that the child was brought to life to bring gifts to offer to the community, to accomplish a particular mission or deliver a specific message to the world. And so, it was the responsibility of the family and the community to help that child discover their purpose. To guide them so that they could clearly understand their path. The same held true on the plantation. My mama named me Ayo because she saw in my eyes that I would walk in and bring joy regardless of my circumstances. I was raised by the community and among many things, they taught me to use my voice to soothe a weary soul. They saw early on that I could take the smallest piece of cloth and turn it into something special, so they showed me how to put pockets on the inside of our clothes for carrying what we needed without anyone knowing what we had. I'd make dolls for our children to have something to call their own and they taught me how to sew messages in quilts so we could talk to one another without words. They guided me to my purpose in life.

So, the questions I have for you are, who is raising your children and what are they teaching them? Have you guided them into being what they were called to do or are they having to figure it out for themselves? Most importantly though, what example are you setting for them?

SCENE 6

Now the second phase of initiation was the rite of adulthood which began around about 13 or so. They would take those young folks away from everybody and everything to teach them how to follow rules and how to look for danger. They taught them to have integrity and pride in themselves and in everything they did. It's when they helped them gain clarity in order that they could fulfill their mission in life. That's when the shaping began in teaching them how to become responsible adults, so they didn't grow up confused.

Now even though we were enslaved, we followed the same guidelines when our children were transitioning from childhood to adulthood. We taught our young folks how to survive by helping them to avoid making the mistakes we'd made. We taught the boys how to be protectors, how to be fathers to the fatherless and to walk like warriors because that was their birthright.

The slavers may have taken our labor, but they couldn't do a thing about how we walked. We taught our girls to know their worth no matter what they were called and to walk in grace no matter the circumstances. I started working when I was about 10 years old and my elders told me, "When you start to make things out of all that good cloth you're given, you make the finest things anybody has ever seen! It'll be your saving grace."

They were right. It kept me with my Matthew for all them years because our work was too valuable, as the Master and Mistress put it, to let us go anywhere. And now we as ancestors look at our kings and queens and wonder, when did we stop loving the naturalness of who we are? When did we start displaying parts of our bodies for all the world to see and give our body no honor? Is the pride in the community and in ourselves gone forever? Mother, fathers, have you provided your children with the tools they need to navigate the ups and downs of life?

SCENE 7

Let me tell y'all something, slavery was one of the most horrendous institutions ever created by man and being on the plantation was brutal on a daily basis. Children were snatched from their mama's arms as she was being sold off, and the beatings were a constant reminder that evil was alive and well. I can remember sewing so much sometimes my fingers lost feeling in them.

Matthew would work the fields, and he was a wheelwright making wooden wagon wheels so, most days he would work from light to dark. Wasn't nothing good about the practice of slavery for us, however, even in the midst of all that pain, suffering and sorrow, we managed to steal moments when we could love on one another anyhow. We'd have gatherings on Sunday, our one day of rest, if the Master and Mistress felt like it, and we would go off in the woods and hold one another, listen to the teachings of our elders, cry out our sorrows, pray for deliverance and dance until our legs would give out. But mostly, ooh we would sing up something!

> She sings a hymn/spiritual or old gospel song like "Every Day'll be Sunday" and does a little dance

Sometimes we'd be out there until the wee hours of the morning and didn't feel no ways tired when it was time to go back to work. Even on the days when they'd almost worked us to death, we would go back to the quarters and tend to our own gardens, work on our own homes, and fellowship together as a family.

We worked hard for our masters and mistresses, but we worked just as hard for ourselves. We were given rations once a week that usually consisted of corn, fruit, pork fat and flour. We had to make that last for a whole week and they didn't care how many folks you had in your household.

I can tell you most of that would run out in the first few days, so in the quarters, there were some that raised chickens, some planted vegetable gardens and others had peas growing. So, after we got our rations, we'd go home and divide up what they gave us and what we'd grown to ensure everybody had enough. Now we weren't perfect by any means and there were some folks that thought the Master and Mistress were good people.

They usually had to learn the hard way. I tried to help them by asking the question, "How can you say a man is good when he can justify the buying and selling of human beings?" I never did hear a good answer for that. Nonetheless, we did all we could to take care of one another. I can't help but wonder what would happen if you all took care of each other like that. I wonder.

SCENE 8

Now, the rite of marriage was the third part of the initiation and that means the uniting of the families and the missions of the couple. They were trained in how to fulfill their destinies together. The priority was on how to build families and how to build communities. Their focus was on the collective and not just themselves. The same held true on the plantation. That's why the field workers, men and women, came up with songs that kept them in rhythm working together to make sure they all made it through the workday.

And when we loved, we loved hard because we didn't know from one day to the next who would be there when we woke up in the morning. Sam had been loaned out to us from another plantation and during the Christmastide he'd get a pass for a few days to go back where he come from. That man would walk thirty miles each way to go see his wife and two daughters. And when he'd come back, we'd have a hardy meal, salve for his feet and I'd make him some new pads for his shoes cause he'd wear them out before he could get his yearly pair. They didn't get to see each other but once or twice a year but they worked all those months in between to prepare for those times.

I remember being told about how my mama and daddy would hold hands every chance they got and in the 75 years me and Matthew was together, we never stopped holding hands either. Even when we didn't like each other too much, we held hands anyway. You see, there's something about the touch of a loved one that can somehow ease whatever you may be going through or pondering over. If you don't believe me, do something for me. If you're with somebody you love, man, woman, or child, take their hand right now.
                    (She encourages the reluctant)
Don't that feel nice? Gives you some security, don't it? Now, let me ask you a questions. And you ain't gotta answer me now, it's just something for you to think on. Like Sam, how far would you walk for the hand you're holding?

SCENE 9

There is an African proverb that says, "each one, teach one," and that brings me to the initiation of eldership in the African tradition. Now this is extremely important because in the elders is where wisdom lies. But what I want you to understand is that just because one gets old doesn't mean they have reached eldership status because they could be old and evil. What it means is that they earned high praise and respect because of the positive impact they had in their community. Their lives were lived purposefully, and they were examples for others to live by.

When I was growing up, there were a few elders on the property, and we younger folks would sit on the floor as they sat in their rocking chairs teaching us all about our history and providing us with life lessons we'd hold on to until we reached eldership. They told stories of the royalty we come from, the beauty of the lands we were born in and the strength of our warriors. They taught us songs, proverbs, bible scriptures they'd learned from those that had been taught to read and write in secrecy. They taught us how to navigate this world we had been forced into and to know that we had to have something to believe in.

They were all strong, but the one that stuck with me the most was Mama Lovie. She'd say in her soft-spoken way, "They can work you; they can beat you, they can take your bodies, but they can't break you unless you allow it. Your mind, heart and soul belong to God and He's the only one that can say who or what you are." She was the one that taught us that love is the way to conquer evil. And that's why I walked in love my whole life because I made up my mind as a young girl, sitting at the feet of Mama Lovie that I wasn't going to let anybody own my heart except by my choosing. Now I ask you, have you given anybody permission to say who or what you are? If you did, just like you gave it, take it back and walk in your purpose!

SCENE 10

Listen here, just one year after my Matthew, I stepped into the last initiation stage of ancestorship. I was able to do so because I lived a purposeful life as a loving wife, a mother to the motherless, and a respected member of my community. As I walked on earth, I walk in the spirit world and that's in love.

Now the reason I can come here and talk with you is because according to our heritage, crossing over doesn't mean the end. Respected ancestors have power and in times of struggle or decision making, know that we are with you and if you call us, we will step forward. Let me tell you something. Since the beginning of time, the Lord has wanted us to do two things. Listen and obey. And since the beginning of time, we as a people have struggled to do so.

My generation and my mama's generation are not the first ones to endure slavery. It has been going on since before the days of Pharaoh and all the times we've gotten ourselves into bondage, it has been because we simply refuse to do what thus saith the Lord. All the instructions you need are right here in the Word. The Lord even sent an example as to how He wanted us to live and still we find ourselves right back where we started.

It is often said that there is nothing that the Lord can't do. Well while that is the truth, there is one thing He has not done up to this point and that's to change the mindset of those that still perpetuate slave-like mentality. We were taught to hate ourselves in every way and to hate one another but that's not who you are. You are a people of strength, love and faith. We were able to endure the middle passage through sheer will and a refusal to be broken.

On the plantation fields we loved deeply in spite of our situations and our faith is what kept us getting up every morning. We didn't bow down to what they called us because we knew who we were and where we come from. We persevered because we knew that one day our children would see freedom and would pass on the stories of our endurance from generation to generation. If y'all could learn to love one another more, you could cure a whole lot of sadness.

This world is in a horrible state of affairs, with walking wounded everywhere, but it's not too late to change things for the better. You can contribute to that change if you start by taking care of you and yours. Cherish your elders, they hold your history and listen to your children cause they hold your futures. We suffered unimaginable things on the journey of enslavement so that you could be the difference our people need.

> Instrumental music plays
> as she asks questions of the
> audience.

So I ask you, will you treat each other better than you've been treated? Will you go spend some time with your parents and grandparents? Will you walk in love? Will you walk into your ancestorship so that when you are called, you too can step forward? Please ma'am, please sir, don't let the work we did go in vain.

> She goes to each of the
> statues and pays homage to
> them before exiting.

END OF PLAY

MEET THE PLAYWRIGHT
Margarette Joyner

Margarette Joyner was born in New Brunswick, N. J. but when asked where she's from she'll tell you she's a nomad. "My mother was a bit of a gypsy; we moved a lot." She did, however, graduate from Miami Northwestern Senior High School and from there joined the military. After a three-year stint in the U.S. Marine Corps, Margarette's first long term job was as a Secretary at the Model City Cultural Arts Center, Miami, FL, under the direction of Marshall L. Davis Sr. It was there that she honed her skills as an artist. She'd taken home economics classes in school and two of the classes she fell in love with were sewing and typing. She brought those talents with her, but once Mr. Davis discovered that her gifts extended beyond one who typed seventy words a minute, he opened any door she asked to enter. It was there that she designed costumes for theatre and dance, acted in stage plays, wrote and directed plays, sang before a large audience, opened for Cicely Tyson, won poetry contests, danced, and created The Tree of Life Theatre Co. and Nandi Creations, all for the first time while remaining a secretary. As a natural talent with no fear, she was often cast in leading roles such as: Colored Museum, Zooman and the Sign, Amen Corner, Ceremonies in Dark Old Men, Big River, God's Trombones, Ghost Stories of the Blacksmith Curse, Wine in the Wilderness, just to name a few. She designed costumes for theatre productions such as: Purlie Victorious, Colored Museum, Santa Goes to Oz and Ain't Misbehavin' for the 'M' Ensemble, Miami's oldest black theatre company. She also designed for The University of Miami Chorale Singers making upwards of 50 dresses singlehandedly. Her powerful voice was called upon often to sing the National Anthem at Fire Station openings, games and various other venues, including the Miami Arena where she sang for the Arise Foundation before 14,000 patrons and sang before 1,100 dignitaries of the United Nations. She was the editor of the Drumbeat Newsletter, and you could often find her poetry in the local newspapers.

After leaving the Center, she went to work for the Dade County School Board to try her hand at a "normal career," having become a single mother. That only lasted a short period of time, because the arts were at her core, and she had inherited her mother's gypsy spirit and moved often. But she knew that if she was going to go to higher heights in the arts, she needed to be formally trained. She was accepted to the University of South Alabama, in Mobile, AL and that is where she received her Bachelor of Fine Arts degree with an emphasis in acting. While there she performed in such productions as Illusions, Cabaret, Eager Beaver Builds a Dam, and A Raisin in the Sun. She also worked in the Costume shop which afforded her the opportunity to spend three summers at The Lost Colony as a costume stitcher, first hand, and Shop Manager, respectively. At the American College Kennedy Center Theatre Festival in Washington D.C. she placed 4th out of some 600 acting students and was awarded a scholarship to Dad's Garage in Atlanta due to her comedic timing, the only undergraduate to place and receive the scholarship. Because of her advanced skills she was asked to design costumes for the theatre department productions of Waiting for Godot, The Reluctant Dragon, and The Laramie Project. Additionally, Ms. Joyner founded the first African American Student Theatre Trope in the history of the school.

After graduating and spending several years as a struggling artist, which included working in costume shops in New York, The Santa Fe Opera and many others, Margarette decided it was time to find a place to call home to give her daughter some stability. She sent out applications all over the country and Richmond, VA answered the call and offered her a job as a Cutter/Draper at Theatre IV, a regional theatre company. She worked there for a decade and was dubbed their "heavy hitter" when it came to complicated and couture garments. Her specialty, however, was in building costumes for, as she puts it, "fluffy" actors. For their children's touring shows she designed costumes for Harriet Tubman, Songs of the Soul, Snow White, Mystery of Ancient Egypt, and Maggie Walker. She also designed costumes and was Prop Master for Cadence Theatre Company, designed for Richmond Triangle Players, African American Repertory Theatre, Henley Street, Firehouse Theatre Project and Fort Lee Playhouse. Additionally, she designed for film companies, Remember Tommy Productions, M.A.M., Inc., and Cadence Theatre documentaries, Sitelines and Bloodlines. She performed for several theatre companies in the area in such productions as: Steel Magnolia, From the Mississippi Delta, Crowns, Best Christmas Pageant Ever, Richard III, Intimate Apparel, For Colored Girls, A Street Car Named Desire, The Bluest Eye, and Blues for Mr. Charlie just to name a few. Realizing that her time had come to leave the organization, she auditioned for an agency that was looking for a Spokesmodel for Glory Foods. Out of 400 auditioners, Margarette landed the role of "Shirley." She was cast for two years to model for print ads in Southern Living Magazine, shoot television commercials, voice radio commercials, appear at green bean challenges and hosted a cooking show. She was also cast in such television series as Mercy Street and House of Cards, documentaries such as Anna, The Green Book Project (which is in the African American Museum in Washington D. C. today), No Ordinary People, VCU Health, and the Smithsonian Project. You can find her in commercials for VA Lottery, Bon Secour, Farley Group Web Series and VA Conservation Association.

When the Spokesmodel job ended, Joyner decided to go back to school. She applied to Virginia Commonwealth University and was accepted and received her Master of Fine Arts degree with an emphasis in Pedagogy within three years. After graduating, she got a job at Virginia Union University, an HBCU as an Adjunct and after 2 years was hired as the only full time faculty member in the theatre department. While being a department of one may have scared the average artist, Margarette embraced it wholeheartedly. For four years she was the Instructor of most of the theatre classes, Academic Advisor for all theater students, implemented an Artist-in-Resident Program by creating The Heritage Ensemble Theatre Co., (THETC), created a full season of shows (producing two shows per semester) with her taking on the responsibilities of Producer, Director and Costume Designer all while teaching five to nine classes per semester. As one could imagine, while rewarding, it was exhausting. With no change in sight, it was once again time to move on. After a brief hiatus, she was hired as an Actor Interpreter at Colonial Williamsburg (CW). While at CW she gave voice to the ancestors of the enslaved community by way of Succordia, an elder and Betty, the cook, both who served the Randolph family. She also gave voice to Charity, the first known free female of color to be admitted to the Eastern Lunatic Asylum in Williamsburg, her most challenging role thus far. While there she wrote and performed one woman shows, directed and created a New Hire Packet. She also continued to design costumes for Richmond theatres for such shows as: Sugar in Our Wounds, How Black Mothers Say I Love You, Vincent River, Shanidar (film), and won an Artsie Award for her design of Fires in the Mirror.

She made a name for herself as a director of shows such as Choir Boy, For Colored Girls..., For Black Boys..., Looking Over the President's Shoulder, Steal Away, When a Woman is Loved Right. She continued to produce, write, direct and costume shows for THETC as well. Plays she wrote and produced are: What They Did For Us, Black Cowboys and Cowgirls, Sweet Chocolate and the Seven Christians (Nominated Best New Play by Richmond Theatre Critics Circle). In addition, she wrote and directed a short film entitled Still Fighting which was entered in several Film Festivals.

One day, while interpreting on the cobble stoned streets, an insensitive guest came to her and asked where he could take his money because he wanted to buy her. Says Joyner, "The work as an interpreter was rewarding in that I had the honor of giving voice to those who had none, however experiencing many incendiary incidents such as this made the job extremely difficult." So once again, it was time to exit. Thankfully, God already had a place in mind for her. One month before turning in her resignation, a theatre professional sent her an email for a job opportunity at the University of North Carolina Charlotte. She interviewed and accepted a two year position of Visiting Assistant Professor of Costume Design. Since her tenure there she earned a grant to write and direct a play based on the ideology of "The New South," designed costumes for SWEAT, Welcome to Our Village, Ring Shout and Clybourne Park. She created a collection of historical garments that span from the 14th to the 20th century by merging African and contemporary textiles embellished with cowry shells which speaks to the royalty of African American people. The collection A Legacy of Elegance was displayed at the DuBois Center's Projective Eye Gallery and then moved to Historic Rosedale, where she is the part-time Program Coordinator and a member of the African American Legacy Project of that historic site. After that, the garments will be exhibited at the Marshall L. Davis Sr. African Heritage Cultural Arts Center, formerly, The Model City Cultural Arts Center, bringing her work back to where it all began.